SKATE-INATOR

Based on the episode "The Beak"
Based on the series created by Dan Povenmire and Jeff "Swampy" Marsh
Story adapted by Michael Teitelbaum

Reader's Digest
Children's Books®

New York, New York • Montréal, Québec • Bath, United Kingdom

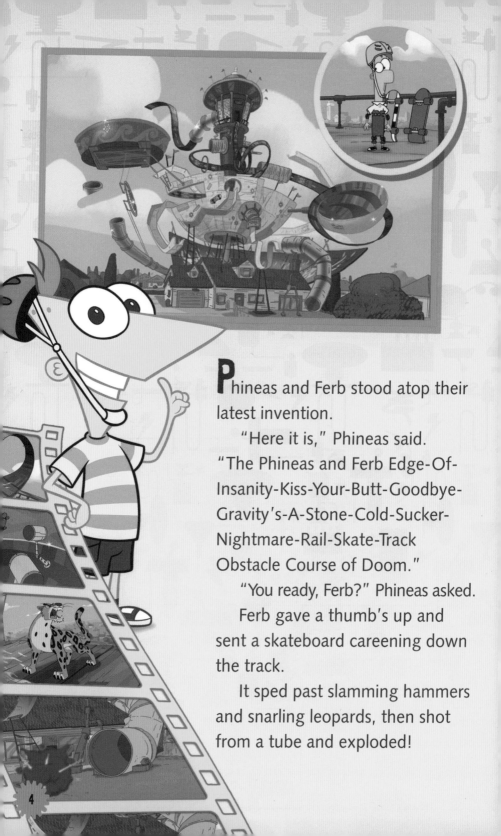

Phineas and Ferb stood atop their latest invention.

"Here it is," Phineas said. "The Phineas and Ferb Edge-Of-Insanity-Kiss-Your-Butt-Goodbye-Gravity's-A-Stone-Cold-Sucker-Nightmare-Rail-Skate-Track Obstacle Course of Doom."

"You ready, Ferb?" Phineas asked.

Ferb gave a thumb's up and sent a skateboard careening down the track.

It sped past slamming hammers and snarling leopards, then shot from a tube and exploded!

"You know, Ferb, it occurs to me we could get hurt," Phineas said.

Meanwhile, the boys' older sister, Candace, searched for her mom so she could bust her brothers for their latest creation. She found her mom at the dentist's office. After Candace's rant about busting her brothers, the dentist said: "Out!"

"Okay, let's get back to your root canal," the dentist said after Candace had left.

"Thank goodness!" Candace's mom said with a sigh.

Just then, Phineas and Ferb's friend, Isabella, walked into the boys' backyard. "Whatcha doin'?" she asked.

"Ferb and I have built the ultimate extreme skate-track obstacle course," Phineas said.

"Awesome!" Isabella exclaimed. She explained she was trying to earn her Fireside Girls Intrepid Reporter Patch. "I knew I could count on you for the coolest story ever! Have you attempted a run yet?"

"Well, we still need to make a few tweaks," Phineas replied. "So we can, you know, survive and stuff."

"Okay, I'll be back in a little while to get the story," Isabella said.

Phineas turned to Ferb. "Instead of modifying the track, maybe we should modify *ourselves*," he suggested. "Together we could be the ultimate skateboarder ever."

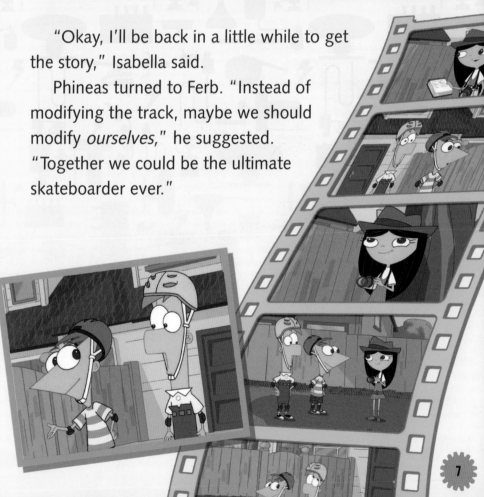

Phineas and Ferb started building a giant metallic skateboarding robot suit that would increase their physical abilities and heighten their senses one hundred times!

When the suit was ready, Phineas climbed into the top half and Ferb strapped himself into the lower half. Together, the boys would control the suit's movements, turning themselves into the ultimate skateboarder.

"How about a little test drive?" Phineas asked.

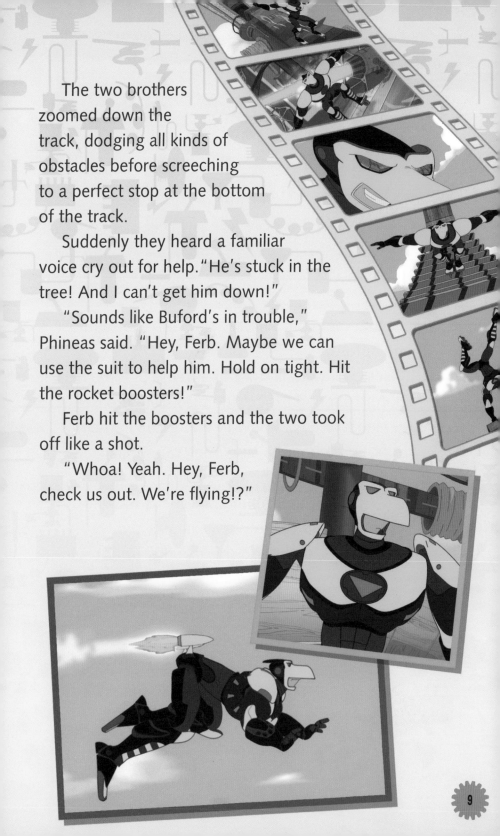

The two brothers zoomed down the track, dodging all kinds of obstacles before screeching to a perfect stop at the bottom of the track.

Suddenly they heard a familiar voice cry out for help. "He's stuck in the tree! And I can't get him down!"

"Sounds like Buford's in trouble," Phineas said. "Hey, Ferb. Maybe we can use the suit to help him. Hold on tight. Hit the rocket boosters!"

Ferb hit the boosters and the two took off like a shot.

"Whoa! Yeah. Hey, Ferb, check us out. We're flying!?"

At that moment, Phineas and Ferb spotted their friend Buford.

"Help, my nerd is stuck in a tree!" Buford cried.

Buford's friend Baljeet tumbled from the tree. But Phineas and Ferb flew to the rescue in their robot skateboarder suit. They caught Baljeet just before he hit the ground.

At that moment, Isabella showed up to interview Phineas and Ferb. Instead she saw their robot suit in action.

"That was amazing!" she cried, snapping a picture of the flying robot. "I can't believe Phineas and Ferb missed it."

Later, in their backyard, the boys got their copy of the *Fireside Girls Gazette*. Phineas read it aloud:

"'Superhero Comes to Danville!' by Isabella Garcia-Shapiro. I call him 'The Beak,'" he read. "Hey, I like that, Ferb! She says, 'With The Beak watching over us, everyone in Danville is free to have the best day ever.'"

Just then, Isabella called. Phineas and Ferb agreed to meet to her downtown for an exclusive interview. Phineas started walking away.

"A-hem," Ferb said, clearing his throat loudly.

"Fine, we can take the suit," Phineas agreed.

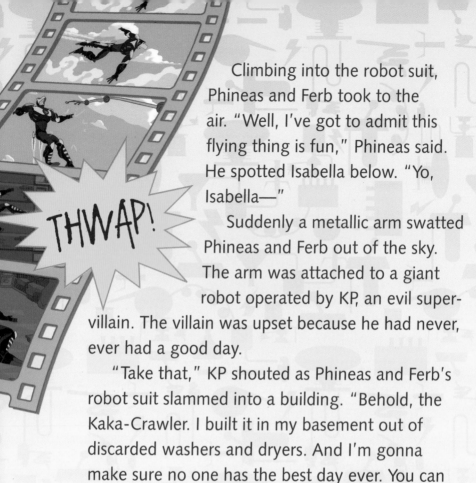

Climbing into the robot suit, Phineas and Ferb took to the air. "Well, I've got to admit this flying thing is fun," Phineas said. He spotted Isabella below. "Yo, Isabella—"

THWAP!

Suddenly a metallic arm swatted Phineas and Ferb out of the sky. The arm was attached to a giant robot operated by KP, an evil super-villain. The villain was upset because he had never, ever had a good day.

"Take that," KP shouted as Phineas and Ferb's robot suit slammed into a building. "Behold, the Kaka-Crawler. I built it in my basement out of discarded washers and dryers. And I'm gonna make sure no one has the best day ever. You can call me: KAKAPOOPOO!"

The Kakapoopoo continued to attack the city. "Who knew wrecking everybody's day would be this much fun!" the evil KP cried.

"Hey you!" shouted Phineas, as he got the Beak suit back up onto its feet and flew into action.

"It's the Beak!" Isabella cried from the street below.

The battle between the Beak and the Kaka-Crawler began—two iron-clad foes clashing in the streets of Danville.

The Beak defeated the Kaka-Crawler, but the evil super-villain vowed to return. "I'll come at you through what's most important to you," he cried as he flew away.

Isabella ran up to the Beak. "Isabella Garcia-Shapiro, *Fireside Girl Gazette.* Can I ask you a few questions?"

Phineas froze. He couldn't let Isabella know that he and Ferb were the Beak. That would put her in danger. "I can't talk right now," said the Beak. Then he flew away.

Meanwhile, Phineas and Ferb had just met up with Isabella. "While you two were busy having fun, other people were busy saving Danville," she said, showing the boys the headlines.

"The Beak, huh?" Phineas commented, pretending he was surprised. "Check it out, Ferb. A real superhero."

"I need your help in finding him," Isabella said. "I thought there might be some clues in the photos I took that could help him stop Kakapoopoo."

Ferb chuckled at the super-villain's name.

A short while later, Kakapoopoo struck again. This time, he poured water on unsuspecting crowds.

"Help me cover the action, Phineas," Isabella yelled from the street below. Phineas was torn. He hated letting Isabella down, but knew he needed to slip away and become the Beak.

"I'm sorry. We can't go with you," Phineas said. Then he and Ferb ran off and put on their robot suit.

"I guess your superhero turned out to be a chicken beak!" Kakapoopoo shouted to the terrified citizens of Danville.

Suddenly, the Beak arrived upon the scene. "Oh, yeah…well, which came first, the chicken or the egg?" the Beak asked as he began firing raw eggs at the super-villain.

"Well, I've got a surprise for you," Kakapoopoo snarled. "I'm not alone. May I introduce 'The Dangeraffe!'"

"Busted!" Candace, as The Dangeraffe, cried out, looking right at the Beak. Candace pretended to be a villain so she could prove Phineas and Ferb were really the Beak.

Phineas grew concerned. It seemed as if Kakapoopoo had Candace. There was only one thing to do.

"I give up," said the Beak. "You win, since you've got her."

"What, *her*? She's just my henchman," Kakapoopoo said.

"I do *not* hench!" Candace shrieked. "Dangeraffe is out. Peace!" Then she stormed away.

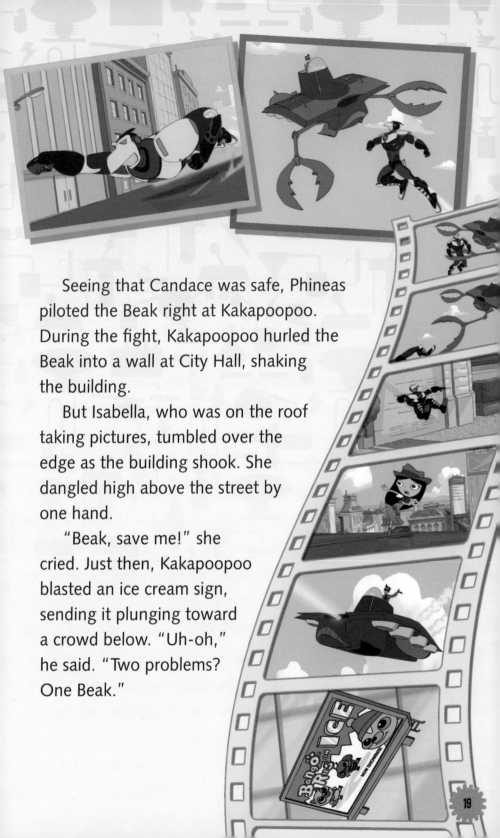

Seeing that Candace was safe, Phineas piloted the Beak right at Kakapoopoo. During the fight, Kakapoopoo hurled the Beak into a wall at City Hall, shaking the building.

But Isabella, who was on the roof taking pictures, tumbled over the edge as the building shook. She dangled high above the street by one hand.

"Beak, save me!" she cried. Just then, Kakapoopoo blasted an ice cream sign, sending it plunging toward a crowd below. "Uh-oh," he said. "Two problems? One Beak."

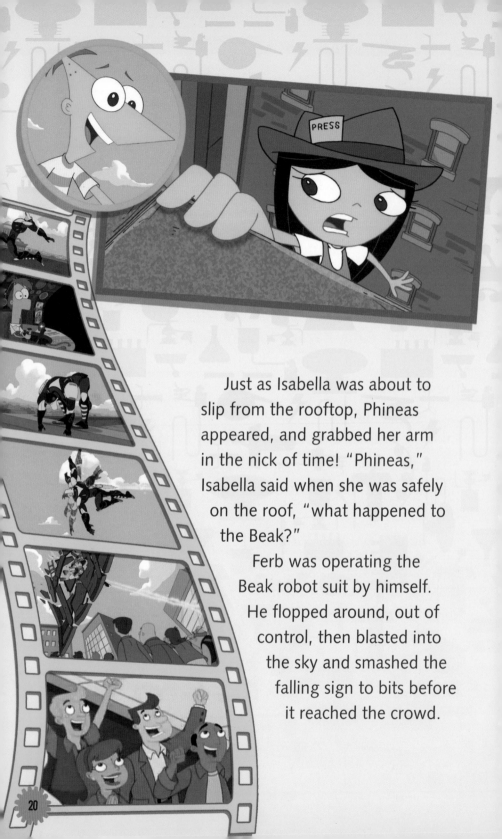

Just as Isabella was about to slip from the rooftop, Phineas appeared, and grabbed her arm in the nick of time! "Phineas," Isabella said when she was safely on the roof, "what happened to the Beak?"

Ferb was operating the Beak robot suit by himself. He flopped around, out of control, then blasted into the sky and smashed the falling sign to bits before it reached the crowd.

Phineas hurried back
into the Beak suit.

"Admit it!"
Kakapoopoo snarled.
"You're having a bad day."

"Never!" the Beak
shouted back. "Nothing's going
to stop me from having the best day ever."

"Well, I've never had a best day ever, thank you
very much!" Kakapoopoo complained.

"I get it, Ferb." Phineas said. "All this guy ever
wanted was to have the best day ever. You know what
we have to do, right?" Phineas and Ferb climbed out of
the Beak costume.

"You're just a couple of kids!" Kakapoopoo cried,
his day ruined once again.

"Phineas is the Beak!" Isabella said in amazement.

"You couldn't tell me because you were protecting me," she realized. Candace's mom stepped onto the street. "Did you see them, Mom?" Candace asked.

"No, I just saw the eye doctor for an exam. Everything's a blurry blob," her mom said.

By the time the Beak was out of sight, her mom's vision had cleared up. "Why don't we all go home for some snacks?" she asked. Everyone cheered.